WITHDRAWN

This is a first edition published in 2020 by Flying Eye Books,
an imprint of Nobrow Ltd. 27 Westgate Street, London E8 3RL.

Written by Stephen Davies and illustrated by Sapo Lendario,
based on the characters and storylines
created by Luke Pearson and Silvergate Media company.

HILDA™ © 2020 Hilda Productions Limited,
a Silvergate Media company

1 3 5 7 9 10 8 6 4 2

Published in the US by Nobrow (US) Inc.

Printed in Great Britain on FSC® certified paper.

ISBN: 978-1-912497-57-7

Order from www.flyingeyebooks.com

CONTENTS

1

Pages rustled. Students bustled. A clock on the wall ticked steadily. Sitting around a table in a corner of the library, noses deep in their books, Hilda, Frida, and David were reading about birds.

The Librarian had given them just the books they needed. Hilda had finished *Feathered Friends of Trolberg* and was already halfway through a terrifying volume entitled *Robber Duckies, Bloodbeaks and Other Birds You Wouldn't Want to Meet*. Frida had written reams of notes on her *A to Z of Every Bird in the World* and did not seem discouraged that she had only reached the letter C. As for David, he was giggling his way through *Fowl Play: A Bumper Book of Bird Jokes.*

"Psst, Hilda," David whispered. "What sort of bird is hard to recognize?"

"I don't know."

"One that's in da skies."

Hilda sighed and returned to her book.

David giggled. "Don't you get it?"

"Of course she gets it," said Frida. "But in da skies and in disguise don't sound similar enough to be funny. Also, none of us are going to get our Birding Badge if you keep da-stracting us from our research."

David leaned back in his chair. "No need to grumble," he said. "I was only—whoa, what's THAT?"

Hilda and Frida followed David's gaze and saw something beautiful fly past the library window: a black bird with a bright red head.

"I've never seen one of those," said Hilda. "Do you know what it is, Frida?"

"It's a super-rare, scarlet-capped warbler!"

said Frida. "If we could get a photo of it, it'd be worth at least ten Birding Badge points with Raven Leader. Have you got your camera with you, David?"

David sighed and pulled his camera out of his satchel.

"Hurry!" Frida urged. "You get the photo and we'll return the books. We'll come and join you in a minute."

David dashed outside and the girls went looking for the re-shelving cart. They found it at the end of Aisle 2 but were surprised to see that it was already overflowing with books.

"That's odd," said Hilda suspiciously. "The Librarian never lets the cart pile up like that. Do you think she's all right?

"Maybe she's helping a customer," suggested Frida, whose imagination had always been a little less wild than Hilda's.

"We can't leave until we know she's okay," said Hilda, rounding the corner and setting off up Aisle 3. "You can come with me or you can go with David."

"And listen to more of his bird jokes?" said Frida. "Not likely."

Up and down the aisles they traipsed, but the Librarian was nowhere to be seen.

"Let's try upstairs." Hilda jumped onto a ladder propped against the shelves. "If I remember correctly, there's a secret reading room on the top floor. What if she's in there?"

"Or what if she's back at her desk after a quick bathroom break?" said Frida, who seemed determined to suggest the most boring of all possibilities.

Hilda walked along Aisle 6 until she came to the

Science section. She gave two sharp kicks at the base of the shelves followed by a swift elbow jab to a large tome entitled *Cryptomechanics*. She knew that this was not a real book at all, but a hidden lever that allowed access to a secret reading room full of spell books.

She had found the secret room by accident a while ago, while researching magical tide mice. Her enchantment of two tide mice had produced unforeseen and traumatic side effects, but (as Hilda often reminded herself) such was the life of an adventurer.

The hidden door in the bookcase swung back, and Hilda stepped through into a dimly lit reading room, which was lined from floor to ceiling with dusty spell books.

"Nobody here," she said gloomily. "You were right, Frida, the Librarian is probably back at her desk."

"Shh." Frida held up a hand for silence. "You hear that?"

Hilda did hear it. The click-clack of high-heeled shoes was quite clear, and it seemed to come from behind the shelves. Hilda hesitated, wondering what to do.

Frida strode to the far wall, knelt down beside a book called *Cauldron Care* and jabbed it smartly with her knuckles. A hidden mechanism clicked and whirred, and two bookcases in front of her slid apart to reveal another room beyond.

"Wow!" gasped Hilda. "The secret room has a secret room. How did you know which book to press?"

"Easy." Frida grinned. "*Cauldron Care* was dusty on top but clean on the spine. Which means that it gets pressed a lot but never gets read."

They ventured further and further into the hidden areas of the library. Secret room after secret room. Hallway after hallway. Staircase after staircase. Most of the staircases were downward ones, and soon the girls realized that they were deep underground.

"I feel bad that David is missing out on this," said Hilda as they wandered along a hallway lined with spell books and strange artifacts.

"Don't feel bad," said Frida. "You know he would have turned back about five secret staircases ago."

The footsteps were suddenly really close. Hilda and Frida dived into an alcove on their left as two women in purple robes rounded a corner at the end of the hallway. They walked straight past the girls' hiding place, deep in conversation.

"Who do you think they are?" whispered Hilda, as soon as the women were out of earshot.

"Isn't it obvious?" Frida replied.
"They're witches. We've stumbled into the most secretive place in all of Trolberg: the legendary Witches' Tower!"

2

"The Witches' Tower?" Hilda goggled at her friend. "But legends and rumors always place the Witches' Tower out in the Huldrawood somewhere."

"Presumably why no one has ever been able to find it," said Frida. "It was underneath the library all along!"

"A tower underground?"

"Of course!" Frida's eyes shone. "It's the last place you'd think to look."

Hilda's mind spun. She had always thought

there was something wonderfully mysterious about the Librarian, and now at last she knew the truth. The Librarian was a witch!

They continued along the corridor, turned right, and passed beneath a foreboding Gothic archway engraved with the words "Hall of Familiars." Framed oil paintings hung along both walls: portraits of notable witches of the past.

"What's a 'familiar'?" Hilda asked.

"A witch's assistant," said Frida. "Often a cat, a frog, or a mouse. Or...er...one of those," she added, pointing to a funny-faced puff dog sitting on the lap of a particularly fierce-looking witch.

Frida looked at the witch in the portrait and then at the engraving on the frame. "Arch-Sorceress Matilda Pilqvist," she read. "Enchanter of Livelihoods, Grand Alchemist of the Dark Communion of Halgar, First

Bloodsister of the Order of the Black Candle, tormentor of—"

"All right, I get it," Hilda interrupted. "She's accomplished and scary. Let's go and find the Librari—aaaargh!"

A door beside the portrait flew open and a dishevelled woman burst out into the hallway. Her black cape streamed behind her and her purple-tinged hair was in a real mess. It was the Librarian, carrying a large, silver sword.

"Gah!" The Librarian stared at Hilda and Frida. "What are you two doing here?"

"We were worried about you," said Hilda.

"Go back, quick!" the Librarian cried. "It's not safe here!"

"Why?"

"There's a triffid behind that door."

"Doesn't sound very scary."

"A triffid is a killer plant."

"Oh," said Hilda. "Okay, that does sound a bit scary."

"I have to face it!" The Librarian glared at the door. "I have to see Matilda Pilqvist, and the

only way to do that is to get through her weird labyrinth, starting with the triffid."

"Why do you need to see her?" Frida asked.

"She has an overdue library book, *The Skeleton Whisperer* by Petra Pakulski. It's overdue by twenty-nine years, three hundred and sixty-four days, and twenty-two hours. Two hours more and it'll be thirty years."

"What happens at thirty years?"

The Librarian lowered her voice to a hoarse whisper. "When a book becomes overdue by thirty years, the keeper of the books gets thrown into the void of no return."

"The keeper of the books." Hilda stared. "That's you."

"Yes."

"You're sure it's not the borrower who gets thrown into the void of no return?"

"No, it's definitely the keeper. The council of high witches will bind me hand and foot and then a bass-playing monster called Lloyd will open the void and throw me in. Sounds unusual, I know, but there it is. Now you understand why I absolutely have to get that book back."

The Librarian lifted her sword and reached for the door handle of Matilda Pilqvist's labyrinth.

"Wait!" cried Hilda. "We'll come with you."

"You?" The Librarian looked them up and down. "But you're just children."

"I know," said Hilda. "But we got this far, didn't we?"

Hilda took the sword out of the Librarian's hand, opened the labyrinth door and stepped inside.

She found herself in a large greenhouse with a vaulted glass ceiling. The room was full of potted plants and there was a heavy oak door at the far end.

The moment they stepped across the threshold, a gigantic plant in the middle of the greenhouse unfurled and came to life. It advanced towards them on leafy tentacle-legs, flailing vicious tendrils like a cat-o'-nine-tails.

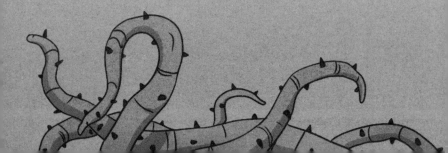

"I'll keep our new plant friend busy," said Hilda. "You two make a run for the door."

"The door is locked," the Librarian said. "I think that triffid must have the key."

Hilda grasped the hilt of the sword in both hands. She swung it fiercely as the killer plant approached, lopping off three flailing tendrils with a single swipe.

The triffid shrank back. Yellow sap oozed from its severed stalks.

As Hilda stepped forward and held out her hand for the key, she noticed something out of the corner of her eye. The three tendrils on the floor at her feet were twitching, sprouting and springing to life.

"Watch out!" called the Librarian. "I should have mentioned, each severed tendril becomes a duplicate of the original plant."

The brand-new triffids were already growing fast, upwards and outwards, unfurling dozens of bright green shoots. They lurched towards Hilda on leafy legs and soon it was impossible to tell which were the new plants and which was the old one.

Hilda took a deep breath and fought with renewed vigor. She ducked and dodged the whip-like fronds, her silver blade went snicker-snack, she lopped and parried like the wind but new plants kept on growing back.

Frida tugged the Librarian's sleeve. "Excuse me," she said. "Is that your own sword or did you find it here?"

"Found it," the Librarian replied. "It was propped up next to the door."

"Thought so," said Frida. "Wish me luck!" She dashed across the greenhouse, snatched the sword from Hilda's hand, limbo-danced under a low-flying tentacle, sprinted to the oak door, and plunged the tip of the sword into the lock.

The sword turned with a satisfying click and the heavy door swung open. In an instant, the crowd of triffids disappeared, leaving just one tired-looking plant in the middle of the greenhouse.

"Frida, that was amazing!" cried Hilda. "How did you know what to do?"

"I noticed a pattern of interlocking keys on the handle," said Frida. "Also, I noticed you weren't really getting anywhere with the plant hacking."

Even the Librarian was gazing at Frida with admiration. "Good work," she said. "If we get through today, I'm definitely going to recommend you for training."

"Training?" Frida gulped. "What sort of training?"

"Witch training, of course," the Librarian said. "You have all the qualities we look for in a young witch. Raw intelligence, coolness under pressure, and incredible powers of observation. Lead on, young Frida! You've got a whole maze in which to practice your skills."

3

While Hilda and Frida were battling the triffid in the Witches' Tower, David was busy with a battle of his own: trying to get a photo of a bird that would not stay still. So far, he had taken six photographs of bits of sky the bird had just vacated, three photographs of branches the bird had just vacated, and one photograph of the top of his own head—which, as bad luck would have it, the bird had just vacated.

He followed the bird through an area of woodland that was in the process of being cleared, ready for new houses to be built.

"TIIIMBERRRR!" called a gruff voice, and a lofty birch tree crashed to the ground right in front of David.

"Hey!" cried a digger driver. "You could have been killed! Get out of here!"

David did as he was told. He clambered over the fallen tree and raced out of the woods as fast as his legs would carry him.

He was not the only one. All kinds of animals seemed to be fleeing the woods and running for their lives. Hares, voles, beavers, squirrels, and pine martens scurried and scuttled, skipped and skedaddled.

The animals emerged onto a grassy plain and scampered into a run-down windmill. The red-headed bird alighted on one of the sails and began to preen itself.

David stopped, regained his breath, then lifted his camera to take a photo.

"Scarlet-capped warbler," said a woman's voice behind him. "Beautiful, isn't it?"

David spun around to see a tall, hooded figure.

"Oh, sorry to disturb you!" he stuttered. "I was trying to photograph it."

The woman pulled down her hood. Lustrous gray curls cascaded around her face. Big eyes shone with intelligence and mischief.

"It's you!" said David.

He had met weather forecaster Victoria van Gale the previous winter, on the day that a terrible snow storm had threatened to bury the city of Trolberg. David and Hilda had visited van Gale at her weather station. What they discovered there was truly disturbing. She was not just forecasting the weather, she was trying to control it.

"Hello, David." Victoria van Gale smiled. "Last time we met, we had a little misunderstanding, didn't we?"

"It wasn't a little misunderstanding," said David. "It was a massive argument. You kidnapped a baby weather spirit for one of your crazy experiments."

"Silly of me," said van Gale. "But I've learned my lesson, David. I've changed."

"You have?"

"Come and see, if you don't believe me."

Van Gale opened the front door of the windmill and led David inside. The interior of the windmill was just as run-down as the exterior, with cracks in the walls and holes in the floorboards. But van Gale had already started to renovate the place. Everywhere David looked, he saw planks, poles, pots of plaster, and rolls of masking tape. He also saw plenty of animals: hares on the chairs, frogs in buckets, and birds absolutely everywhere.

"After my weather station was destroyed, I moved in here," van Gale said. "I'm fixing the place up, and I've also taken in some animals and birds from that awful housing development down the road. Poor little things." She reached out to a red squirrel on a step ladder and tickled it under the chin.

David scowled. "Are you doing experiments on these animals?"

"Of course not!" Victoria van Gale looked shocked. "I'm simply offering them a safe place to live."

There was a loud splintering sound and a big

crack appeared in the far wall of the windmill.

"Oh dear," van Gale sighed. "This place is falling apart around my ears. Every time I fix one thing, something else goes wrong. If anyone tells you it's easy to make a ruined windmill into a cozy home, don't believe them." She glanced at her watch and forced a smile. "Anyway, enough about me. You photograph that scarlet-capped warbler, and I'll check on my baking. I've got a batch of pastries in the oven."

David went outside and found the scarlet-capped warbler was still sitting on the sails of the windmill. He raised his camera to one eye and was about to take the photo when an ecstatic yip filled the air and a deer fox bounded into view, a furry white bundle of courage and cuteness, closely followed by Hilda and Frida. The warbler was startled and flew away.

"Did you get the photo?" shouted Frida.

"No, I didn't, thanks to Twig. How did you know I was here?"

Frida grinned. "Your shoes have a very distinctive zigzag pattern on the sole."

"You tracked my footprints?" David said. "I didn't know that was one of your skills."

"It is," said Hilda, "and that's not even the most impressive thing that Frida has done this afternoon. She's also dodged a killer plant, used a sword as a key, answered seven sphinx riddles, spotted an invisible glass floor for crossing a pit of spikes, concocted a glass of pineapple punch for a genie, navigated a reverse-perspective tunnel maze, crossed a salt lion moat in the belly of a surgeonfish, beaten a fire monster in a game of chess, retrieved an overdue library book from an arch-sorceress, and helped her find her kettle. Oh, and she also saved the Librarian from being cast into the void of no return."

David frowned and wiped his nose on his sleeve. "Frida did all that while I was trying to photograph one bird?"

"Yes." Hilda beamed. "And when we finally reached Matilda Pilqvist's house, she told us that many seasoned witches have failed to get through her labyrinth. She was so impressed, she volunteered herself as Frida's personal trainer."

Hilda lowered her voice to an excited whisper. "Frida's going to learn magic, David. She's going to be a witch!"

"I see." David gulped. "Plenty more petrifying adventures in store for us, then."

A sudden scream of terror filled the air, making all three children jump. But it was only a pine marten being chased through the long grass by Twig.

"Stop that, Twig." Hilda scooped him up into her arms.

"Look at all these cute animals," said Frida. "They're everywhere!"

"David!" called a voice inside the windmill. "The pastries are ready. Come and get them while they're hot!"

Hilda gasped. "That voice," she said. "It sounds like—"

"Victoria van Gale." David nodded grimly. "She says she's turned over a new leaf. She says she's set up home in this ruined windmill and is converting it into an animal sanctuary."

"Aww!" Hilda put her hand on her heart.

"That's so sweet."

"Yes, well, I don't believe her for a second," said David. "Once a mad scientist, always a mad scientist, that's what I say."

"What do you suspect she's doing?" asked Frida.

"I don't know. But whatever it is, I'll bet you it's something completely loopy."

"And what are you going to do about it?"

"I'll tell you what I'm going to do about it." David clenched his fists. "I'm going to go inside, I'm going to eat two pastries, maybe three, and I'm going to offer to help Victoria van Gale with her renovation project. That'll give me the chance to nose around a bit and find out what she's up to."

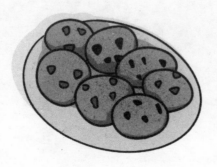

4

"Hi Mom, I'm home!" Hilda barged in through the front door and pulled off her red rubber boots. The apartment was toasty warm, as always, and a divine aroma of ginger, nutmeg, and caraway seeds wafted over her.

"Hilda!" Mom jumped up from her desk. "You took such a long time. Where were you?"

"At the library," said Hilda, "and then at the windmill. They're turning it into a refuge for animals from the housing development."

She deliberately did not mention the fact that the "they" in question was actually Victoria van Gale. Mom had borne a grudge against van Gale ever since the weather station incident, and she would not be happy about Hilda having anything to do with her.

"How lovely." Mom went into the kitchen and came back with two steaming bowls of stew. "I hate to see trees being cut down to make room for yet more houses."

Hilda leaned close to her bowl and gobbled her stew. She was no longer thinking about the windmill, but about today's adventures with Frida in the Witches' Tower, and their conversation with Matilda Pilqvist. Not only had the arch-sorceress offered to be Frida's teacher, she had also recommended Hilda as Frida's familiar. Just think of that—a witch's assistant!

After dinner, Hilda gathered up the bowls and took them to the sink. The kitchen was unusually tidy, with bare, gleaming surfaces.

"What's going on?" said Hilda.

"Where is everything?"

"Looks nice, doesn't it?" grinned Mom. "Tontu offered to store half of our kitchen stuff in Nowhere Space for us. It's freed up all our countertops!"

Tontu was a nisse, or house spirit, who had taken up residence in Hilda's flat.

"Very generous of him," Hilda muttered. "It's a pity he's not so generous when it comes to letting us actually travel through Nowhere Space."

"I heard that," said a disembodied voice. "Nowhere Space is a sacred space, I'll have you know, and it's not meant for humans. I should never have taken you there in the first place."

As soon as Hilda and Mom finished washing the dishes, they settled down in the living room to play the boardgame Dragon Panic. Hilda got off to a slow start. Her village was on a mountaintop and it took forever to gather supplies. But when the dragons started arriving, she was glad of her high location. Her archers fended off attack after attack, while Mom's settlement was burned to a crisp.

"Well done," said Mom, slumping back against the sofa cushions. "You played cleverly tonight."

"Let's play again," said Hilda.

"No chance!"

"Just one more, please!"

"No," said Mom, reaching for the TV remote. "You can watch five minutes of *Trolberg Tonight* and then you're going straight to bed."

The TV screen flickered to life. Linn Jacobsen, presenter of *Trolberg Tonight*, was looking even graver than usual. "The fishing ship was called the

Nimbus," she was saying. "All four crew members are missing, presumed drowned."

"Oh no," said Mom. "It sounds like another ship has sunk."

"It can't have!" cried Hilda. "That's the fourth sinking this week!"

"Citizens of Trolberg are understandably anxious about the recent spate of sinkings," Jacobsen continued. "Perhaps our next guest can shed some light on the matter. Commander Erik Ahlberg, welcome to *Trolberg Tonight*."

"Thank you for having me," said a nasal voice, and the camera zoomed in on the smug, fleshy face of Erik Ahlberg. He was wearing the brown and yellow uniform of the Trolberg Safety Patrol, complete with a jaunty feather in his hat.

"Who wears a feathered hat indoors?" said Mom.

"Someone who is a teeny bit bald and incredibly vain," said Hilda. "I can't believe they asked him onto *Trolberg Tonight* to talk about the sinkings. He'll find a way to blame it on trolls, just you wait."

"Commander Ahlberg," the interviewer began, "you have been investigating the recent sinkings in Björg Fjord. Who or what do you think—?"

"Trolls," interrupted Erik Ahlberg. "Legend has it that certain species of troll are able to survive underwater as well as on land. These amphibious beasts are wandering our fjord, as cool as sea cucumbers, occasionally reaching up to pluck a ship out of the water and devour its crew."

"And what solution do you propose?"

"I bet he says bells," muttered Hilda.

"Bells," said Ahlberg. "Enormous, underwater bells, and plenty of them."

Linn Jacobsen raised her eyebrows. "Do bells work under water?"

"Perfectly." Erik Ahlberg twirled his thin moustache. "Some of your viewers may not be aware of this, Linn, but there is already one such bell on the seabed near Trolberg harbor. It is five hundred years old and had never been rung in living memory, but my men tested it last week and its ding-dong is as clear and loud as any modern bell." Ahlberg turned to the camera and spoke directly into the lens. "Make no mistake, dear viewer. That underwater bell and others like it are needed more than ever in these dark days."

"He's not thinking straight!" cried Hilda. "He thinks trolls are behind everything bad that happens. If his airship ran out of fuel, he'd blame trolls. If his toast fell on the floor butter-side down, he'd blame trolls. If a pigeon pooed on that stupid hat of his, he'd blame—"

"Not so loud, Hilda!" Mom said. "I agree, he does seem a little obsessed with trolls, but who knows, perhaps he's right this time."

"Amphibious trolls?" Hilda snorted. "Come on, Mom, there is zero evidence that they even exist. The explorer Emil Gammelplassen wrote about that legend in his new book *Fjords and their Unfriendly Occupants* and he called it the silliest legend in the history of silly legends."

Mom pursed her lips and turned her attention back to *Trolberg Tonight*, on which Ahlberg was now taking phone-in questions from members of the public.

The first caller was a fisherman who had

worked in Trolberg harbor for more than fifty years. "Ahoy there, Ahlberg!" he roared down the line. "I been listenin' to you landlubbers gassin' about trolls, but we seadogs know best. There be only one beastie in the fjord that could've scuttled those ships."

"And which beastie might that be?" Ahlberg asked.

The silence that followed was so long that Hilda thought the fisherman had rung off. But it turned out he was only pausing for effect. "That there Lindworm on Cauldron Island," he said, rolling his r's dramatically. "A mangy, scurvy, coldhearted devil if ever there was one."

5

The next morning, Hilda sat at the breakfast table with her head on her chin, wondering what to do. Everyone else seemed to have plans for the day. David was at the windmill helping Victoria van Gale with her renovation project. Frida had gone to the library for her first witching lesson with Matilda Pilqvist. Mom was working at her desk. And as for Alfur, her elf friend, he was away all week, having been summoned back to the wilderness for a three-day grammar conference. Today was Day Three of the conference, which (if Hilda remembered the program correctly) was entitled Fun with Fronted Adverbials.

"Come on, boy," said Hilda to Twig. "Let's go down to the harbor and see what's going on there. Maybe we can find some clue to the sinkings of those ships."

She finished her porridge, pulled on her boots, and set off running through the streets of Trolberg. Her yellow scarf streamed behind her and Twig gambolled at her heels, just like old times.

At the entrance to the harbor was a bar called The Salty Maiden, and as Hilda passed it, she was startled by the noise of breaking glass. A big wooden log smashed through the front window of the bar and landed on the cobblestones outside.

"And don't come back, ye worm-eaten knave!" roared a voice from inside the bar.

Hilda looked closer and realized that the log was not a log at all. It was a book-loving, guitar-playing, forest-dwelling wise guy who Hilda liked to believe was her friend.

"Wood Man!" Hilda hurried up to him. "You poor thing! Are you all right?"

"I won a game of dice," said the Wood Man, gazing up at the bar with large, expressionless eyes. "The sailors at The Salty Maiden love a game of Sea Bones, but they don't love it if you try to leave straight after winning a fully rigged sailing ship."

"You shouldn't gamble," said Hilda. "And you shouldn't visit Trolberg without coming to see me and Mom. You don't even have to knock, you know. Just walk right in, like you used to. Oh, Wood Man, I've got SO MUCH to tell you."

"That's what I was afraid of," said the Wood Man, and he turned and walked away.

"Hey!" Hilda hurried after him. "Where are you going?"

"I'm going out to sea," he said. "I need to leave now if I'm to find the Draugen by sunset."

"Okay…" Hilda almost had to run to keep pace with the Wood Man. "Wait, what's a Draugen?"

"Draugen, plural, are the spirits of drowned sailors, doomed to sail on a ghost ship for all eternity."

"And you want to find them?"

"Yes."

"Good thinking," said Hilda. "The Draugen are sure to know what's been causing the sinkings. Can I come with you?"

"No."

They arrived at the waterfront and stared up at a large sailing boat with the name *Nautilus* stenciled on its hull. It was tied to a mooring post and its pristine white sails were fluttering in the breeze.

"Nice ship," said Hilda. "No wonder they

chucked you through that window. You'll have a hard time sailing it on your own, though."

The Wood Man considered this. "Fine," he said at last. "You can come if you want to."

Ten minutes later they were traversing the harbor with the wind in their sails, weaving among yachts, schooners, dingies, and skiffs. The Wood Man stood at the helm, holding the wheel. Twig performed lookout duty on the foredeck. Hilda stood at the stern and watched a family of salt lions playing in their wake.

A good south wind sprang up behind the ship, carrying them past Cauldron Island and out into the open sea.

"Deckhand!" called the Wood Man. "Tighten the main sheet!"

"Huh?" said Hilda.

"And ease off the vang!"

"Eh?" said Hilda.

The Wood Man heaved a weary sigh. "Pull the big rope and loosen the little one."

"Sure!"

As Hilda hurried to adjust the ropes, a massive

albatross glided over her head. Hilda thought
of her Birding Badge and she wished she had a
camera with her to get a good, clear shot of the
feathered giant.

"Tacking south-south-east!" the Wood Man
called. "Heading for that eerie patch of mist on
the horizon!"

This seemed like a sensible idea. All of the
ghost ships in Hilda's picture books at home were
wreathed in an eerie mist. Why should the Draugen's
ship be any different?

Sure enough, the Wood Man was right. The
moment they entered the mist, the wind dropped and
the sails of the *Nautilus* hung slack. Twig lowered
his antlers and his tail fluffed up to twice its normal
size. As for the friendly albatross, it let out an ear-
piercing caw and doubled back as if sensing danger.

Then there it was, looming out of the fog towards
them. A tattered sail. A rotting hull. Two masts like
brittle bones.

"Wood Man," said Hilda, doing her best to
keep her voice low and level. "I think we've found
the Draugen."

The ghost ship drew alongside the *Nautilus*, and a seaweed-covered gangplank slid into position. Hilda, the Wood Man, and Twig walked across it.

Slimy, many-legged creatures scuttled across the deck of the Draugen ship. But it was the crew that really fascinated Hilda. Stiff armed, stiff legged, and weirdly translucent, they lowered the tattered sail and dropped an anchor.

"Ahoy me swabbies!" cried a throaty voice, and a skinny ghost appeared in front of them. "I'm Nicholas, the First Mate," he added, in a much less throaty voice. "Have some Draugen grog."

A brimming mug appeared in Hilda's hand, but when she sipped it, she realized it was basically just sea water.

"Thank you," said Hilda, reminding herself that it was the thought that counted.

"Meet our captain," said the First Mate, stepping aside.

The Draugen captain was a ghastly sight. Bony wrists and hands poked out from the wide sleeves of her tattered overcoat, and a jaunty crest of

seaweed clung to her ghostly scalp. Also, for some reason Hilda could not imagine, there was a metal hook embedded in the captain's right shin.

"Sorry about the grog," the captain chuckled. "Our real grog ran out some time ago."

Before long, they were chatting like old friends. The captain told Hilda all about the Draugen's free-roaming, swashbuckling adventures aboard their ghost ship, and Hilda began to feel that perhaps being a Draugen was not such a cursed existence after all.

"Do you know anything about the recent sinkings in the fjord?" Hilda asked.

"No idea," said the captain. "Our ship is always wreathed in this blasted mist. We can't see a thing!"

There was a sudden commotion below deck and a Draugen sailor appeared, carrying the Wood Man under one arm. Hilda had been so engrossed in the captain's stories, she hadn't realized that the Wood Man had slipped away.

"Caught this one red-handed," said the sailor. "He was trying to steal our magic coral sextant."

"I wanted it for my dining room," said the Wood Man tonelessly. "I'm giving it a nautical theme."

6

Back in Trolberg, David was struggling with sails of a different sort. Windmill sails.

Victoria van Gale had given him a delicious breakfast of cinnamon rolls and then assigned him his first renovation job: loosening the jammed sails of the windmill.

"Just clean the dirt out of the middle bit," she had said. "You'll have them spinning in no time."

As it turned out, van Gale's breezy optimism had not been well founded. David had inched himself up the sails with great difficulty and was now perched just above the central dial, paralyzed with fear and clinging on for dear life.

"Put your hand in the gap between the sprockets and the drive chain," van Gale shouted from the ground. "Find whatever gunk is stopping the sails from turning."

David had no desire to find gunk of any sort, but now that he was up here, he had to do something. He reached his left arm into the mechanism and started pulling out cobwebs, dead leaves and nauseating slime.

"Why does an animal refuge need moving sails?" he shouted.

"Renewable energy," van Gale yelled back. "I'll use the wind to power my lights, heaters, TV, kettle, toaster, rice cooker, pressure cooker, slow cooker, cake mixer, ruby laser, waffle iron—"

"Wait." David frowned. "What's a ruby laser?"

"Did I say ruby laser?" Van Gale laughed awkwardly. "Slip of the tongue. I meant smoothie maker. In fact, I think I'll go and make us some smoothies right now. Call me when the sails are working!"

"All right." David pulled out another handful of gunk, then another, then twelve more. The central dial creaked and quivered.

"There!" David yanked from the gap one final clump of filth. "Aaaaaargh!" he added, as a sudden gust of wind caught the sails and blew them all the way round.

David flattened himself against the wooden slats and held on tight. He was on his side, then upside down, and then the right way up again.

"Help!" he screamed. "The sails are turning!"

"Well done, David!" Van Gale's voice from inside the windmill sounded muffled but cheerful. "That's wonderful!"

"Not wonderful!" shrieked David, turning upside down again. "Not wonderful at all! Help me!"

But it was too late. David lost his grip, plummeted through the air, and landed (as luck would have it) in a leafy rowanberry bush.

"Ouch," he said, crawling out of the bush on his hands and knees.

Then he heard it—a weird chuckle from around the side of the windmill. David turned his head and saw a flash of movement, as if someone or something had dodged back out of sight.

"Victoria?" David got to his feet. "Is that you?" But even as he said it, he knew that the weird chuckle he had heard was not from a human.

BANG!

What was that? A door being slammed by the wind? Or something else?

His heart pounding, David tiptoed around the outer wall of the windmill. On the far side, he found a low wooden hatch that looked like the entrance to a cellar.

He gripped the edge of the hatch and heaved it open, revealing a flight of stone steps descending into darkness. Whatever had been spying on him had almost certainly gone down there.

David would not normally have dreamed of investigating a dark, scary cellar by himself. But today was different. He had to find out what Victoria van Gale was up to, and this was his best clue so far. Sick with dread, he climbed through the hatch and tiptoed down the cold, stone steps.

The cellar was pitch black and smelled of mold. David edged forward with his arms out in front of him, his trembling fingers touching sacks of potatoes here, a broken wheelbarrow there, and sticky cobwebs all over the place.

A cockroach skittered suddenly across his foot, causing him to yelp in fright and blunder sideways into a shelf. Jars smashed. Tins clattered. Matches and candles rolled.

Matches! Candles! David felt around and picked them up.

The first four matches he tried were soggy and useless. The fifth one flickered and went out. The sixth one worked.

"Hello?" David lit a candle and raised it in front of him. "Is anybody there?"

Silence.

He inched forward, peering into the shifting shadows at the edge of the candlelight. "I know you're there," he quavered. "Show yourself!"

Stacked against the far wall of the cellar was a mound of broken furniture. David held the candle high above his head and narrowed his eyes to help him see.

In amongst the odds and ends lay a number of strange-looking mannequins, or at least, bits of mannequins. Here an arm and there a leg. Here a body, there a head. Not one of these weird dolls was complete.

Except for one.

The mannequin that attracted David's attention looked like it was made of moss. It had been discarded upside down on the side of the heap, a funny-looking figure with a pot belly, four stubby limbs and a giant, bulbous head. It looked a bit like a nisse.

David bent low over the mannequin, shining the candlelight across its face. It was the eyes that really fascinated him. At the center of each eye was a tiny pinprick of light, as if those dark pupils were actually reflecting the flame of David's candle. Very impressive workmanship.

David stared at the mossy mannequin and the mossy mannequin stared back at him.

And then it blinked.

"Aaaargh!" shrieked David, dropping the candle.

"Raaargh!" cried the creature, leaping to its feet and flinging itself at David, its eyes alive with rage.

The candle hit the floor, snuffing itself out and plunging the cellar into darkness. David turned to run but the creature was too fast for him. It tackled him around the waist, dragging him down onto the mound of mannequins.

"Get off me!" cried David, craning his neck away from the creature's snapping teeth.

Click.

A shaft of light appeared above and a coiled

rope tumbled through it.

"Grab on!" called Victoria van Gale.

David seized the rope and felt himself being whisked out of the creature's clutches, up, up, up and into the light. Victoria van Gale hauled him through a trap door onto the living room carpet and slammed the hatch behind him.

"Phew, that was close!" Van Gale double-locked the hatch and covered it with a dust sheet. "You met my assistant, then?"

David sat up, blinking in the light. "If your assistant is a creepy mannequin made of moss that attacks people for no reason, then yes, I met your assistant."

Van Gale sighed. "He does get a little grabby when he's startled. But most of the time he's completely harmless. I built him to help me with the renovations."

"You built him?"

"Yes." Victoria van Gale smiled. "I knew I was going to need some help renovating the windmill, so I made a little nisse to assist me. Do you like him?"

7

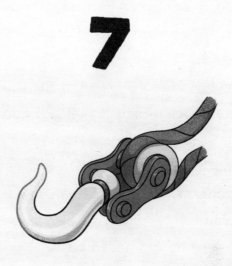

Dangling off the side of a ghost ship in the middle of Björg Fjord, an enormous iron hook lowered towards the ocean with three very anxious captives attached to it. The rope creaked as it descended inch by inch.

"Sorry this is taking so long," the captain called. "We're short on winch oil."

"Take your time," muttered the Wood Man.

Hilda strained against the ropes. "Wood Man, this is all your fault," she whispered. "You said you wanted to find out about the sinkings in the fjord."

"Actually, it was you who wanted that," said the Wood Man. "I just wanted a Draugen sextant. Is that so shellfish?"

"Absolutely!" Hilda glanced at the waves below, where ferocious salt lions leapt and snapped their jaws.

"Captain," shouted Hilda. "Do you always turn your captives into Draugen, or is there some sort of alternative?"

"Sorry," the captain yelled back. "No alternative."

The Draugen first mate cleared his throat. "Except—"

"Nicholas!" snapped the captain. "Don't you dare."

"There is one alternative," the first mate gabbled. "Tradition dictates that if the captive sailors can beat the Draugen in a race back to harbor, they should be freed at once." The first mate looked startled by his own words and he clapped a hand over his mouth.

The captain sighed and looked down at her captives. "I'm guessing you're challenging us to a race, then."

"Yes!" yelled Hilda.

"Sure," said the Wood Man. "Why not?"

The Draugen hauled up the metal hook inch by inch, and allowed their captives to return to their ship.

Both crews set about preparing for the race. They raised sails, adjusted knots, and tightened lines. As soon as the ships were ready, one of the Draugen sailors launched a flare, which exploded—BANG!—into the shimmering shape of a ghostly skull.

"GO, GO, GO!" the Draugen captain cried.

The ships plunged forward, bow to bow. It seemed for a moment that the *Nautilus* had the edge, but then the Draugen ship suddenly zoomed ahead, ghostly energy churning in its wake.

"They're using magic!" cried Hilda. "That's cheating!"

"They did seem rather confident for people with holes in their sails," the Wood Man noted.

Hilda glanced up and saw a weather spirit hovering above them, watching the race with interest.

"Hi there!" called Hilda. "Could you follow along behind us, please? We could do with an extra puff of wind in our sails."

"No chance," said the weather spirit.

"Why not?"

"Because a weather spirit is a force of nature," huffed the spirit. "Not a servant to little girls."

Hilda sighed. The Draugen ship was already half a mile ahead. The race was as good as lost.

"It doesn't matter," said the Wood Man in a

loud whisper. "It doesn't look like it's got much puff in it anyway."

The weather spirit turned dark purple. "I heard that!"

"Looks a little wispy, if you ask me," whispered the Wood Man.

"Wispy!" The weather spirit huffed and puffed. "I have never been so offended in all my life. Blue-haired girl, tell your captain to apologize this instant!"

The sails of the *Nautilus* twitched, and an idea popped into Hilda's head.

"Don't take it personally!" Hilda yelled to the weather spirit. "Wood Man here is rude to everyone. Besides, he's not the captain of this ship."

"Really?" The weather spirit drifted closer. "What is he?"

"He's the captain's log."

"Haha," the weather spirit chortled. "The captain's log! Good one!" Puffs of wind from the spirit's chuckles filled the sails of the *Nautilus* and nudged it forward in the water.

"When we first set sail," said Hilda, "the Wood Man's girlfriend came to the harbor to wave him off. 'Bring me back a diamond necklace!' she called. 'Sure!' he called back. 'I'll bring you back a diamond—but don't call me Neckless!'"

"Neckless! Hahaha!" The weather spirit burst out laughing, powering the *Nautilus* forward past Cauldron Island.

"Last week we landed on a tropical island," shouted Hilda. "The inhabitants wanted to crown the Wood Man their king. They said he'd make an excellent ruler."

"Bahahahaha!" The weather spirit laughed like a drain. "He would indeed. He'd make dozens of excellent rulers!"

The ship surged forward, faster and faster, drenching Hilda and Wood Man with sea spray. The spirit followed close behind, eager for another joke.

"What's the Wood Man's least favorite month?" shouted Hilda.

"I don't know."

"Sep-TIIIMBERRRR!"

The weather spirit roared with laughter, releasing yet more wind. They were moving powerfully through the water and gaining on the ghost ship. Hilda could see the Draugen captain at the wheel, her seaweed hair streaming behind her in the wind.

"What does the Wood Man wear on his left foot?" Hilda shouted up to the weather spirit. She paused for a moment and then yelled, "Wooden shoe like to know!"

The *Nautilus* was level with the ghost ship, ploughing through the water with astounding speed. They were almost back at The Salty Maiden.

"What did the beaver say to the Wood Man?" yelled Hilda. "Nice gnawing you!"

"PAHAHAHAHAHAHAHAAAAA!" A final gale of laughter burst out of the helpless spirit and into the sails of the *Nautilus*. The ship shot across the harbor, veered sharply to starboard, and crashed into the dock so hard that Hilda, Twig, and the Wood Man were thrown clean off the ship's deck and onto the quay.

A split second later, the ghost ship arrived at high speed, colliding with the starboard fender of the *Nautilus*. Hilda expected the hulls of both ships to splinter like matchwood, but the prow of the Draugen ship passed right through the *Nautilus* like a ghost through furniture.

"You hornswogglers!" The Draugen captain shook her fist and cracked a rueful grin. "You won't beat us next time!"

The ghostly sailors turned their ship around and headed back to sea. Hilda jumped to her feet

and waved at them.

"Goodbye," she called, "and thank you for the grog!"

The Draugen adjusted their tattered sails, drifted across the harbor and vanished into mist.

"One more joke," the weather spirit pleaded. "Just one more joke, then I'll be on my way."

"All right," grinned Hilda. "Knock-knock."

"Who's there?"

"Definitely not the Wood Man."

The weather spirit pulled a face.

"The Wood Man never knocks," Hilda explained. "So if you hear knock-knock, you can be pretty sure it's not the Wood Man."

"I don't find that funny in the slightest," said the weather spirit stiffly. "Goodbye."

And with that, it flounced away.

8

Hilda ran all the way to the library with Twig at her heels. When she arrived, she found Frida in one of the secret reading rooms, waving her hands over a cockroach. Frida looked up with a start, and goggled at her friend's wet clothes and disheveled hair.

"I went sailing with the Wood Man," Hilda explained. "We were almost killed and turned into Draugen but I managed to save the day by telling jokes to a weather spirit. How was your morning?"

"Okay... Well, I had my first witching lesson

with Tildy," said Frida. "She taught me something called psychobiokinesis and then she gave me an assignment. I'm supposed to form a strong mental connection with another living thing."

"A cockroach?"

"I thought it would be easier to start with something small." Frida scowled at the critter on the table. "I don't even know if it's working."

"Maybe you could try with Twig," suggested Hilda.

Twig whined nervously and backed away.

"Another time," smiled Frida. "Let's go and find David, shall we?"

David was outside Victoria van Gale's windmill, putting up a bird box.

"David!" yelled Hilda. "How's the renovation going?"

David jumped at the sudden greeting and accidentally bashed his thumb with a hammer.

"OW!" he yelled. "Don't creep up on me like that! And for your information," (he dropped his voice to an urgent whisper) "it's not going well at all—not even a teeny-weeny-little-bit well. Victoria van Gale has confirmed all of my worst suspicions about her."

He told them about the creepy basement beneath the windmill and the strange creature that attacked him there.

Hilda shrugged. "Why shouldn't van Gale create a fake nisse thingy to help her out? It must be ever so lonely out here all on her own."

"That's right," Frida added, "and anyway, just think how many Sparrow Scout badges you're going to earn for your work here: renovation, interior design, care for animals, birding—"

"Yoo-hoo!" called van Gale, emerging from the windmill. "David, I've made us some cucumber sandwiches—" She broke off when she saw Hilda and Frida. "I'm sorry, I didn't realize we had visitors. Hello, girls."

"We've met before," said Hilda, shaking hands. "During the storm, remember?"

"Ah, yes." Van Gale's breezy smile deserted her for an instant, then quickly reappeared. "Tell me something," she said. "Do you like cucumber sandwiches?"

"We love them!" cried Hilda and Frida
in unison.

Five minutes later, Hilda, Frida, and
Victoria van Gale were lounging on moth-eaten
armchairs inside the windmill, munching cucumber
sandwiches and listening to an eerie song on
the radio.

*"Down in the middle of the Iron Pine Forest
there's a pile of screaming stones,*

*Down in the middle of the Iron Pine Forest
there's a pile of gleaming bones."*

David went paler and paler with every line of the song, and he grew even more anxious when van Gale's weird nisse came out of the kitchen with a tray and started serving drinks.

"Keep that thing away from me!" he snapped.

Hilda peered at the creature with interest. "What's it made from, Victoria?"

"Oh, you know." Van Gale gestured vaguely. "Moss and hair and other bits and bobs. You could make your own if you wanted to."

"Maybe I will," said Hilda. "My current nisse is pretty useless, to be honest. He doesn't even let me into Nowhere Space any more."

"Wait, what?" Van Gale leaned forward and had a weird glint in her eyes. "You've been in Nowhere Space?"

"Hundreds of times," said Hilda, which was a major exaggeration.

"Fascinating." Van Gale licked her lips. "David,

why don't you show Frida the bug hotel you've been working on? Go on, I can tell she really wants to see it!"

David and Frida exchanged a confused look but they went outside. As soon as they were gone, Victoria van Gale fetched Hilda a notebook and a packet of felt-tip pens.

"Do you like drawing?" she asked.

Hilda nodded.

"Draw me something nice," said van Gale. "I know! Why not have a go at drawing Nowhere Space?"

Hilda chose a purple pen. Slowly and carefully, she drew a wobble-walled tunnel lined with glowing holes.

"Astounding," breathed van Gale. "Tell me, Hilda, did you use a quantum accelerator to enter?"

"A what? No. I just held my nisse Tontu's hand."

"How narrow was the entry point?"

Hilda frowned, "Pretty narrow, why do you ask?"

"As narrow as that?" Van Gale flung out an arm to indicate the crack in the wall behind her.

At that moment they were interrupted by the return of David and Frida.

"Very nice," Frida was saying. "Although to tell the truth, David, your head was already a perfectly good bug hotel."

Van Gale pocketed Hilda's diagram and called her assistant to bring more cordial.

"We should give him a name," said Hilda. "How about Moss Head Fred?"

"Or Evil Steve," muttered David darkly.

"I prefer Hilda's suggestion," said van Gale.

At one o'clock, the lunchtime news came on the radio. "Another fishing boat has sunk in Björg Fjord," the newsreader said. "It went down near Cauldron Island at approximately ten thirty this morning. Rescue boats are searching the area, but no survivors have been found."

Hilda shook her head. "I don't believe it," she said. "That's the fifth sinking this week!"

The newsreader continued. "Erik Ahlberg of the Trolberg Safety Patrol is now blaming the sinkings on the Lindworm of Cauldron Island.

He is putting together a marine strike force to capture the Lindworm and put an end to these all-too-regular tragedies."

Hilda jumped to her feet and shouted at the radio. "This is not right!" she cried. "There's no way the Lindworm is involved. David, Frida, we need to go down to the harbor right this minute and stop him launching those Safety Patrol boats."

"How are you going to do that?" asked Victoria van Gale.

"I don't know," said Hilda, "but the Sparrow Scout Oath is all about being kind to all animals, people, and spirits, and that includes the Lindworm. We can't let Erik Ahlberg attack her!"

David shook his head. "I'll be with you in spirit," he said, "but right now I'm very busy being kind to these animals right here." He pointed at a family of voles asleep in a cardboard box.

"Right," said Hilda, doubtfully. "What about you, Frida? Will you accompany me on this potentially traumatic adventure?"

Frida smiled up at her blue-haired friend. "Wouldn't miss it for the world," she said.

9

Hilda and Frida rode their bikes all the way
down to the harbor and locked them up at The
Salty Maiden's bike rack. The quayside was a
very different place to the one Hilda had left
two hours ago. Now it was buzzing with activity.
Twelve Safety Patrol boats were being fitted out
with harpoons, ready for battle. Commander Erik
Ahlberg himself strode along the quay, barking
orders at clusters of nervous-looking sailors.

"Excuse me, Mr Ahlberg," said Hilda.

Ahlberg looked down at her with the expression of a man who has just found a slug in his salad.

"Please don't attack the Lindworm," said Hilda. "We've met her, and she's a gentle, peace-loving soul. She would never attack a boat. All she wants is to be left alone to tend her garden."

"The experts disagree with you," said Ahlberg curtly. "Now, if you'll excuse me, I have a million and one things to attend to." With that, he strode off along the quay, inspecting the Safety Patrol boats and barking orders.

As Hilda stared after him, she suddenly felt very small and powerless.

"If we can't stop the strike force," said Frida, "we can at least warn the Lindworm that they're coming for her."

Hilda scanned the harbor and noticed the *Nautilus* still moored at the end of the quay beyond the Safety Patrol boats. "The Wood Man's ship!" she cried. "Come on!"

They sprinted along the quay towards the ship. Frida and Twig ran straight down the gangplank onto the deck. Hilda untied the rope from the

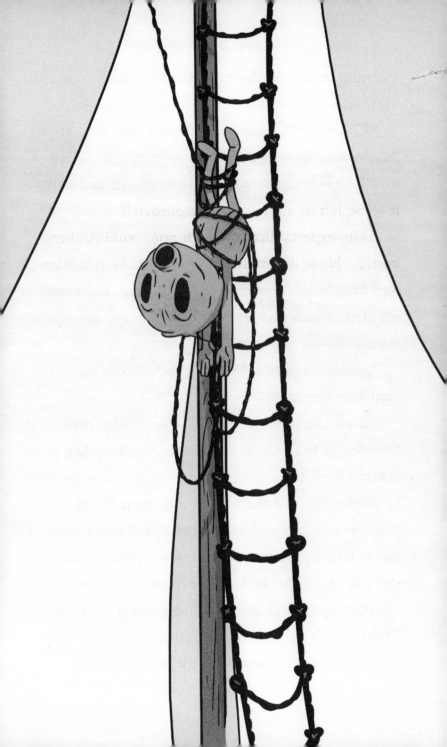

mooring post, then boarded the ship with a giant leap.

"Charming!" cried a doleful voice that seemed to come from somewhere up above.

Hilda shielded her eyes from the sun and saw the tiny figure of the Wood Man perched way up high at the top of the rigging. He was swaying to and fro in the breeze like a bee on a dandelion.

"Charming!" he repeated. "I climb the futtocks to mend a sail, and no sooner do I reach the top than someone steals my ship!"

"Sorry!" yelled Hilda. "We didn't think you were here!"

"That's fine, then," said the Wood Man, his voice dripping with sarcasm. "So long as a person is absent, it's totally acceptable to make off with their property. Where are we going, anyway?"

"Cauldron Island!" Hilda yelled. "Ahlberg is about to attack it with twelve Safety Patrol boats."

"Typical." The Wood Man started to climb down the rigging. "We're going to an island that's about to get blown to smithereens. The perfect day out."

As Cauldron Island came into view, Hilda

spotted a wisp of purple smoke coiling into the sky
from the garden at the center of the island.

The Wood Man alighted on the deck.

"Nice to meet you, Wood Man," said Frida.
"Any friend of Hilda's is a friend of mine."

The Wood Man gazed back at her with empty
eyes. "You clearly have more confidence in Hilda's
judgement than I do."

When they arrived on the shore of the island,
the Wood Man stayed with the ship while the
others jumped down onto the white, pebbly beach.

Twig seemed delighted to be back on Cauldron
Island. He led Hilda and Frida up over the rocks
and down through the hidden valley beyond. He
skipped over lilac bushes, nibbled at wild sage, and
dived joyfully in and out of giant roffleworts.

Before long, they reached the Lindworm's lair.
The slender dragon was sitting in the middle of
the clearing, using a pair of tiny scissors to trim a
miniature tree.

"Hello!" said Hilda.

The Lindworm reared up tall and sucked
great gulps of air into her hydrogen glands,

preparing to frazzle the intruders to a crisp. Then her eyes widened in recognition and her body relaxed a little.

"Oh, it's you," said the Lindworm, bending low. "Have you come to give me more city plant specimens?"

"No," said Hilda. "We've come to get you off this island. The commander of the Safety Patrol thinks you've been attacking ships in the fjord."

"He's mistaken," said the Lindworm. "I've been right here all week, trimming my *ficus benjamina*." She pointed at the tiny tree. "Weeping figs make excellent miniatures, don't you think?"

"Forget your weeping fig," said Frida. "You'll be a weeping Lindworm if you don't get off this island quick."

The Lindworm tossed her proud head. "I'm not scared," she said.

"You should be," said Frida. "Ahlberg has twelve boats and hundreds of harpoons."

The Lindworm reared up on her haunches, her massive nostrils quivering with rage. "I am a Lindworm!" she cried, "and I live by a code, which is never to back down from a battle. If it's a fight they want, then it's a fight they'll get. They'll soon regret picking on a fire-breathing dragon who suffers from social anxiety!"

And with that, she turned tail and slithered off into the trees.

"Come back!" called Hilda. "Come with us on our ship! You can make a home for yourself in the Great Forest. It has all kinds of gorgeous plants!"

Frida slipped her hand into Hilda's. "Let's go," she whispered. "We can't help her if she doesn't want to be helped."

Hilda's heart ached as she trudged back to the beach with Frida. Even Twig walked with his tail turned down, sensing their sadness.

When they reached the top of the valley and looked out to sea, they could not believe their eyes. The *Nautilus* had left without them.

There it was, in the middle of the fjord, tacking north towards the harbor with a fair wind in its sails. From where Hilda stood, the Wood Man was no more than a tiny speck on the foredeck.

"Hey!" yelled Hilda. "We're still here! You've left us behind!"

Then she saw the reason for the Wood Man's swift departure. Ahlberg's fleet had set sail and was heading across the fjord towards Cauldron Island, harpoon cannons at the ready.

"I thought you said the Wood Man was your

friend," Frida muttered.

"It's complicated," said Hilda.

No sooner were the words out of her mouth than the *Nautilus* pitched violently to starboard and disappeared beneath the waves.

10

"Wood Man!" yelled Hilda, breaking into a run. Tide-smoothed pebbles clacked beneath her feet as she sprinted down the beach into the foaming surf.

A mesmerising tone vibrated in the air. Hilda turned around and saw that Frida was holding a hefty, pale-blue conch shell to her lips. The bugle call swelled to a crescendo, reaching out across the fjord.

WHOOSH! A tall column of water rose up in front of the girls. Two watery eyes blinked open.

"Oh," said the water spirit, "it's you."

It was the second time today that Hilda had heard the phrase "Oh, it's you" in a disappointed tone of voice. But this was not the moment to complain about such things.

"Water spirit, you've got to help us!" Hilda begged. "Our ship has been sucked under the sea and our friend the Wood Man is on board!"

"Trivial problems," sighed the water spirit, but it let down its staircase all the same.

Hilda, Frida, and Twig ran up the staircase and perched on the spirit's head.

"Where exactly did the ship sink?" the spirit asked, as it raced across the surface of the fjord.

Hilda considered this, and then had to admit that she had absolutely no idea.

It was Frida who came to the rescue. "Carry on north," she said. "Now east a bit... and a bit more... and stop!"

Hilda stared at her friend in wonder. "You memorized the precise location!" she said. "Did Matilda Pilqvist teach you how to do that? Is it some kind of ancient witching art?"

"No." Frida slid into the sea and held up a

coconut. "I spotted this thing floating in the sea, that's all."

Hilda leaped down to join her friend, entering the fjord with a great splash. She gasped at the coldness of the water, and then she gasped a second time, because the thing in Frida's hand was not a coconut. It was the Wood Man's head!

"Well, this is awkward," said the Wood Man's head.

"It certainly is," said Hilda. "I can't believe you left us."

"Ha," said the Wood Man.

"We could have died."

"Hahaha," said the Wood Man.

"And now you've lost your body."

"Hahahahahahaha!" said the Wood Man.

"Wood Man, why are you laughing?"

"There's something tickling my feet," said the Wood Man. "I don't even know where my feet are right now, but they're definitely being tickled."

"Did you see the thing that sank your ship?"

"All I saw was two enormous tentacles," said the Wood Man. "I tried to outpace them, but it was impossible. One tentacle grabbed the ship, another grabbed my body, and hahahahaha."

At the mention of tentacles, a cold shiver ran down Hilda's spine—although that might also have had something to do with the temperature of the fjord.

"Now I get it," said Hilda. "The Wood Man didn't leave us behind on purpose. His ship was being attacked."

Frida looked unconvinced, but she said nothing.

"Thanks for your help," Hilda said to the water spirit. "Could you take our deer-fox friend back to the harbor, so we can stay here with the Wood Man's head and search for the tentacled monster that's tickling his feet?"

"Wow," said the water spirit. "There's a sentence that's never been said before."

It turned to leave, then stopped. "Will you need to swim underwater?"

Hilda nodded.

"Hold still, then." The spirit reached out a watery hand and slapped Hilda gently around the face, enveloping her head in a silvery bubble

the size of a diver's helmet. Then it did the same
for Frida.

"Do you want one, too?" the water spirit asked
the Wood Man. "Or are you going to quit while
you're a head?"

"Very funny," muttered the Wood Man.
"And yes, I would also like a bubble helmet."

"Say please."

"Please."

The water spirit slapped Wood Man hard around the face, encasing his head in a third magic bubble. Then it zoomed off across the bay, chuckling to itself. Hilda saw Twig's ears flapping in the wind as he disappeared into the distance.

"Wait for us on the quayside, Twig!" yelled Hilda. "We'll be back soon!"

Frida put her face in the water. "These bubble helmets are amazing," she said. "We can open our eyes, and breathe, and even talk!"

"Pity," murmured the Wood Man's head.

"Come on, Frida," Hilda cried. "Race you to the seabed!"

Hilda flipped her legs up above her head and propelled herself straight down with long, powerful dolphin kicks. Frida tucked the Wood Man's head under one arm and followed as quickly as she could.

At first there was nothing to see—just chilly green water all around—but as the girls went deeper and deeper, an underwater paradise revealed itself in all its beautiful weirdness. Jellyfish pulsated. Octopodes inflated. A smirking spiny dogfish glided past. Fluorescent yellow sea slugs oscillated their antennae while a school of orange stingrays nibbled clams.

On the seabed far below, Hilda spotted a graveyard of sunken ships. They looked as if they had once been magnificent vessels, with sleek wooden hulls and beautifully carved prows.

"Whoa!" said Hilda, diving down to the ships. "Look at these!"

"I'd love to," muttered the Wood Man, "but I'm facing into your friend's armpit."

"Sorry," said Frida, turning the Wood Man's head around so he could see.

"Oh, that," said the Wood Man. "That's the remains of a pirate battle many moons ago. It has nothing to do with this week's sinkings."

Hilda snapped a rotting handle off a ship's wheel and handed it to Frida. "Found you a wand," she said.

They swam on through fabulous coral formations shaped like brains, fans, and deer-fox antlers. They swam past cross-looking crabs and graceful turtles. They even swam through a kelp forest, feeling their way forward through the thick, wavy fronds.

On the far side of the kelp forest, Hilda stopped dead, gaping in amazement at the thing in front of her. Standing upright on the seabed, suspended within a giant metal frame, was a gigantic bell. It was rigged with cables, which Hilda guessed were connected to a control booth somewhere in Trolberg harbor.

As they watched, the cables twitched and the bell burst into life with an ear-splitting underwater BONG!

Fish scattered. Anemones retracted. Lobsters poked their heads back into their holes.

"Whoa!" shouted Frida. "What is that massive bell doing down here?"

"It's here to drive away amphibious trolls," said Hilda. "Ahlberg said he tested the bell last week, but it looks like he's doing more than that. He's ringing it regularly!"

The last echoes of the bell died away and a bizarre creature swam into view. It looked to Hilda like a cross between a jellyfish and a cow, with stubby tentacles and wide, dopey eyes.

"Look!" cried Frida. "It's the monster that sank the *Nautilus*!"

"Don't be silly," said Hilda. "It's nowhere near big enough for that."

"I'm not talking about the baby." Frida craned her neck upwards, her face a mask of horror. "I'm talking about the mom!"

11

Back at the windmill, the day's renovation work
was nearly complete. Birds chirped in bird boxes,
bugs scuttled in the bug hotel, squirrels chattered,
frogs played leapfrog, chipmunks chased their
tails, and the majestic windmill sails went round
and round.

At four o'clock in the afternoon, Victoria van
Gale went into town to buy supplies, leaving
David to complete the final task of the day—
filling in the various cracks that snaked across
the windmill's inner walls. He poured five cups of

powdered plaster into a bowl, added a splash of water, and stirred the mixture with a knife to make a thick, creamy paste. When it was ready, he got to work, slapping the paste into cracks in the wall and smoothing it over with a scraper. He worked quickly and quietly, glancing over his shoulder occasionally to check that Moss Head Fred was not about to attack him again. Being left on his own with the creature made him feel more than a little nervous.

To be fair, Moss Head Fred had behaved quite well this afternoon. He watched David's plastering with interest and even tried to help, dipping his own scraper into the plaster and attempting to fill a crack. But his movements were too jerky and he ended up flinging the plaster in David's face instead of at the wall.

Eventually they found a way to cooperate. Moss Head Fred held the bowl and David did the actual filling and smoothing. They worked their way around the windmill until only one crack remained—a deep fissure in the east wall. Victoria van Gale had left them strict instructions not to fill in this particular crack. She said she wanted it to be a home for woodlice.

Moss Head Fred put down the bowl and went outside. David wandered over to the bookcase, hoping to find a storybook to read while he waited for van Gale's return. Unfortunately, all of the books were science-themed: chemistry, physics, biology, geology, laser technology, necromancy...

Wait! Necromancy? Wasn't that something to do with bringing dead things back to life?

David ran a finger along the titles in the necromancy section: *Creating Life (The Hard Way)*, *Playing God for Experts*, *Reanimation: A Comprehensive Guide* and *The Walking Meat*.

He took *The Walking Meat* off the shelf and stared at it in horror. Why was van Gale so interested in necromancy? He looked around him at the strange windmill, filled with birds and beasts and creepy-crawlies. In the fading light, it was all beginning to look horribly creepy.

David was about to replace the book when he noticed a tightly bound scroll in the shelf space behind. He picked it up and unrolled it with trembling fingers.

At the top of the scroll were a dozen mathematical equations, then a diagram of a windmill with an odd-looking stick poking out of the top. The stick was labelled "lightning conductor" and seemed to be connected to the sails of the windmill, which were in turn connected to a "quantum accelerator" and a "ruby laser." David tried to remember where he had heard those phrases before.

When he opened the scroll a little further, a piece of paper dropped out. On it was a drawing in purple pen, labeled with the phrases "entry point" and "Nowhere Space." David glanced

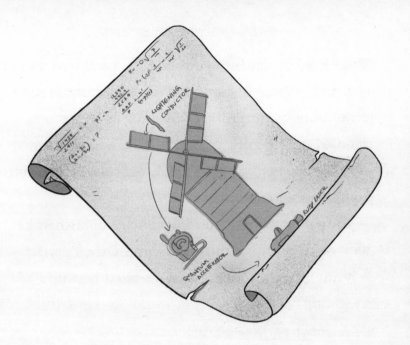

up at the crack in the wall and a terrifying idea occurred to him.

What if that crack was not for woodlice?

Something behind him cleared its throat. Moss Head Fred was staring at the scroll in David's hands.

"I've really enjoyed working with you, Fred," stammered David, "but I've just remembered, it's bath night tonight, so I'd better run."

He pushed past the nisse and made a dash for the door. He nearly made it, too, but Moss

Head Fred caught up with him at the last second and tackled him around the waist, slamming him to the floor. A dozen birds rose off their perches, squawking in fright.

"Get off me!" yelled David. "Let go of me, you pestiferous puppet!"

Moss Head Fred was shorter than David but also remarkably strong. He bound David's wrists and ankles with garden twine, picked him up like a rag doll, and carried him to the iron post in the center of the windmill.

"Good knotting technique," said David, as Moss Head Fred tied him to the post with yet more garden twine. "You'd make an excellent Sparrow Scout if you weren't, you know, awful."

With the knots all checked and double-checked, the creature shambled out into the dusk in search of van Gale.

David was left alone. At least, he thought he was alone, until he noticed that one of the rabbits cowering under the coffee table was carrying something on its back—a little elf with a pointy hat.

"Coo-ee, David!" called the elf. "You seem to be in a bit of a pickle."

"Alfur!" cried David. "What are you doing here? I thought you were at a grammar conference."

"It ended this afternoon," said Alfur. "When I got back home, I couldn't find Hilda anywhere. Mom told me that she might be here."

"You just missed her," said David. "She and Frida went down to the harbor to save the Lindworm, whilst I stayed here and got attacked by Victoria van Gale's moss monster. I found some secret plans, Alfur. Van Gale is planning to use a ruby laser and a quantum accelerator to open a

massive portal into Nowhere Space!"

"Interesting," said Alfur. "Why did you choose 'whilst' instead of 'while'?"

"What?" said David. "How is that the interesting part of what I just said?"

"Because we were discussing it at the conference only this morning!" said Alfur. "Most grammarians agree that 'while' is more up to date than 'whilst', and also less pretentious. No offense."

At that moment, Moss Head Fred returned. He had not managed to find van Gale but he had managed to find a big pointy stick. He pulled up a chair and sat on it, glaring at his hostage.

"Cut me loose," said David loudly. "There's a knife in the plaster bowl on the floor by the wall."

Moss Head Fred shook his mossy head.

Alfur ran over to the plaster bowl. He jumped up, grabbed the end of the knife and swung on it.

The knife did not budge.

"Okay, forget that idea," said David. "Go to the harbor and fetch Hilda and Frida. Tell them to come quick!"

Moss Head Fred shook his head again and pointed his pointy stick towards David's chest, as if to say, Be quiet or else.

Alfur climbed up David's clothes and into his inner ear. "That's another interesting one," he whispered. "'come quickly' is correct, of course, but your 'come quick' is so commonly used that you could probably make an argument for its acceptability. It all depends on whether you see grammar as prescriptive or descriptive. If you're asking for my opinion on the matter—"

"Just do it!"

Alfur did as he was told. He jumped down to the floor, leaped onto his buck-toothed steed, and rode off towards the harbor.

12

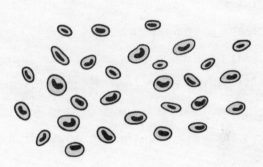

Hilda stared up at the sea monster. Beneath a sun-bleached shell, a barnacle-covered body pulsated grotesquely. Eight gnarly tentacles wriggled and writhed. Dozens of yellow eyes kept unblinking watch on their surroundings.

No words could do justice to the sheer bulk of the thing. It was bigger than massive, bigger than gigantic, bigger than colossal. Although it was at least two hundred yards away from Hilda and Frida, its tentacles were so gargantuan, it could easily have reached out and grabbed them.

"Okaaay," said Hilda. "Mission accomplished. Perhaps we should go back up to the surface now."

"Definitely." Frida's voice came out like a squeak.

"Good plan," said the Wood Man's head. "Who needs a body, anyway?"

Up and up they swam, using their feet like flippers to propel them towards the surface. Compelled by a mixture of fear and fascination, they kept their eyes on the many-eyed monster the whole way up.

"Look," said Hilda, pointing. "It's so humongous, it pokes up above the surface of the water. I can see waves breaking on its shell."

"You're right," said Frida. "What I don't understand is, how come we didn't see it from Cauldron Island?"

Hilda reached the surface first and her bubble helmet burst with a soft pop. The sun was setting in the west and the pebbles on the beach of Cauldron Island shone glorious shades of pink, purple, orange, and red.

Hilda frowned, then gasped out loud.

"Frida, get up here quick!" she yelled. "There's a very good reason why we didn't spot the monster's shell from Cauldron Island. It's because the monster's shell *is* Cauldron Island!"

As Hilda gaped at the rocky island, she was reminded of Bobblehat Mountain near her old house in the wilderness. That mountain had turned out not to be a mountain at all but an ancient Giant that had fallen asleep thousands of years ago.

Had the gargantuan sea monster in front of her also been asleep for millennia? Hilda imagined the natural deposits of sand, rock, and vegetation that could accumulate during such a long period of time, creating a habitat where all sorts of flora and fauna could thrive.

"It's called a Kraken," said a doleful voice in Hilda's ear. The Wood Man's head was bobbing on the waves between her and Frida.

"A what?"

"A Kraken," said the Wood Man's head. "But according to legend, it should be asleep for another hundred and seventy-five years."

"Wait," said Hilda. "You knew this thing existed?"

"Of course. Didn't you?"

"No!"

"You should read more," said the Wood Man.

"That massive bell must have woken the Kraken," said Frida. "Remember, Ahlberg sent out Safety Patrol divers to test it six days ago, which was exactly when the sinkings began."

"You're right!" cried Hilda, excitedly. "We have to tell Ahlberg."

"You can do it now if you like," the Wood Man said. "He's right behind you."

Hilda turned and saw the prow of a Safety Patrol motor boat bearing down on them. It missed them narrowly and continued towards Cauldron Island.

"We're coming for you, Lindworm!" shrieked a nasal voice. "You can run but you can't hide!"

"She can hide, sir," came the voice of Gerda Gustav, Ahlberg's Safety Patrol deputy. "She can run and she can also hide. We hear she's very good at both."

Another boat soared past, then several more. There were twelve boats in all, some made of wood and some of metal. Hilda and Frida waved and yelled, but the Safety Patrol officers did not see them. They were focused instead on Cauldron Island, staring in mingled terror and excitement at the Lindworm that had appeared on a rocky slope.

The girls watched the bold dragon slither towards the oncoming ships. They watched her rear up on her back legs and suck three massive gulps of air into her hydrogen glands, preparing to fight fire with fire.

"Harpoons at the ready!" Ahlberg yelled.

A black cannon stood on the deck of each Safety Patrol boat. Officers busied themselves priming the cannons, inserting a long spear into the muzzle of each one.

Hilda swam after the boats. "Don't fire!" she yelled. "The Lindworm is innocent! We have proof!"

"FIRE!" bellowed Ahlberg.

With a thunderous boom, the twelve harpoons exploded out of the cannons. High into the air they sailed, their ropes unfurling behind them.

All twelve splashed harmlessly into the water on the far side of Cauldron Island.

"Wow," said Frida. "They're not very good shots, are they?"

The enraged dragon thrust its long neck forward and blew a fantastic jet of fire towards the boats, causing the seawater between them to roil and hiss. Steam drifted across the water, stinging

Hilda's eyes and throat.

"Reload!" bawled Ahlberg. "Lower all cannons by five degrees!"

Hilda and Frida swam on into the churning chaos of the battlefield. "Lindworm!" cried Hilda. "Lindworm! Over here!"

"FIRE!" thundered Ahlberg.

Again the harpoon cannons boomed.

Again the vicious spears soared high into the air.

Again the Lindworm sucked in air to belch a scorching jet of flame. But then, quite unexpectedly, the dragon paused. She had spotted a little blue-haired girl struggling in the waves.

"Hello, you!" the dragon called. "Hardly an ideal place for a swim, if you don't mind my saying."

"The island is a Kraken!" yelled Hilda at the top of her voice.

The Lindworm cupped a clawed hand to one ear. "You feel a little shaken?" she queried. "Don't we all, my dear!"

Hilda tried again.

"THE. ISLAND. IS. A. KRAKEN!"

This time the dragon understood. As harpoons rained down on the island, the Lindworm made a great leap forward, plunging into the surf with an almighty crash.

The harpoons missed the Lindworm but pierced the Kraken's shell. A cloud of bubbles fizzed up to the surface of the fjord—a howl of indignation from the titan of the deep.

"Oh no," said Hilda. "Now they've done it."

Rocks clashed. Seashells cracked. Pebbles on the beach vibrated ominously. The whole of Cauldron Island was shaken to its foundations and then, with a shuddering groan like the end of the world, the harpoon ropes twanged tight and the Kraken reared up from the sea.

Tentacles waved. Yellow eyes glared. Slimy mouthparts slobbered and gnashed. The Kraken of Björg Fjord was well and truly awake, and she was furious.

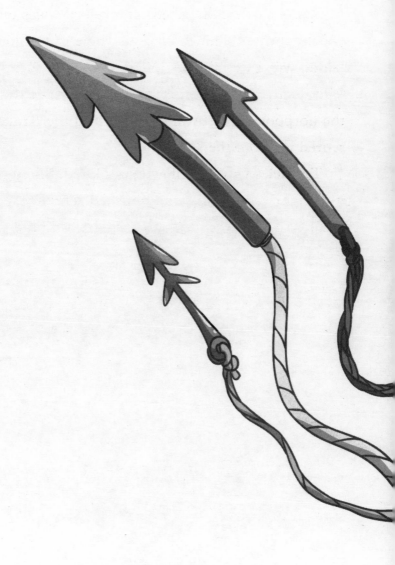

13

Immense volumes of sea water continued to cascade off the island's rim as the Kraken ascended majestically into an indigo sky. The Safety Patrol boats, still connected to the monster by the triple-strength harpoon ropes, began to rise up out of the fjord.

"Disengage harpoons!" cried a frantic Erik Ahlberg, but it was too late. The keels of the twelve boats were already clear of the water and the harpoon operators were tumbling head over heels down the sloping decks.

"Abandon ship!" squawked Ahlberg, letting go of the wheel and flopping backwards into the sea.

All twelve patrol boats dangled above the water, bobbing and spinning in mid-air like corks on a wide-brimmed hat. As Hilda watched in horror, a monstrous tentacle breached the surface of the sea, curled itself tightly around one of the wooden boats and plunged back down beneath the waves.

"Oi!" bellowed Erik Ahlberg. "That's my boat! Give it back!"

Hilda and Frida put their faces in the water to see what the Kraken would do with the boat. They soon had their answer. A tentacle reached down towards a crimson coral shelf and dropped the wooden boat into a nest of baby Krakens.

The babies were small but ravenous. They tore the boat apart and wolfed it down in seconds.

Another boat followed, then a third, a fourth and a fifth.

"Look," said Hilda. "The momma is offering them some wooden boats and some metal ones, but the babies are only eating the wooden ones."

"Picky eaters," smiled Frida. "If only we could

tell the momma Kraken that there is an all-you-can-eat buffet of wooden pirate ships right beneath her. Then she wouldn't need to grab fishing boats and Wood Man bodies and suchlike."

Hilda nodded excitedly. "Maybe there is a way to tell her. You could use that thing you've been learning—forming a mental connection with another living thing."

"Psychobiokinesis?"

"That's the one! If you were able to point the Kraken towards the delicious ship graveyard, perhaps it would leave the Safety Patrol boats in peace."

"All right." A gleam of determination appeared in Frida's eyes. "I'll try."

Frida headed for the Kraken, slicing through the water with lithe fish kicks. But as soon as she got close, a blue-gray tentacle whipped towards her and seized her around the waist.

"Stay calm!" Hilda yelled. "Use your magic."

Frida closed her eyes and laid her hands on the coiled tentacle.

"Have you still got that stick we took from the

sunken ship?" Hilda yelled. "You could use it as a wand."

Frida pulled the stick from underneath her sweater and stroked it back and forth against the Kraken's gnarly skin.

"Concentrate!" yelled Hilda. "Block out all distractions!"

Frida opened her eyes and shot her friend an exasperated look.

"Sorry!" yelled Hilda.

Frida closed her eyes again. Hilda could only imagine the mental strain of trying to link minds with an ancient sea monster. But after a minute or two, a serene smile appeared on Frida's face and the tentacle around her body seemed to relax a little.

"What's it saying?" yelled Hilda, frustrated at being left out of the conversation. "And what are you saying? And what is it saying back? And what are you saying to that?"

"Hang on, Hilda," Frida murmured.

Ever so gradually, the Kraken lowered itself back down into the sea. An extra-long tentacle reached into the inky depths of the fjord and came back up with the wreck of a wooden pirate ship. It fed the wreck to the babies on the coral shelf and they reacted with bubbly squeals of pleasure and excitement.

"Look at that," said Hilda. "I guess old ships are tastier than new ones."

The tentacle reached once more into the babies' nest, pulled out a headless doll and passed it to Frida.

"Aw, cute," said Hilda. "The Kraken gave Frida a doll."

"That's no dolly," said a morose voice close at hand. "That's my body."

It did not take long for Cauldron Island to return to its normal position, with the tide lapping quietly against its pebbled beach. Nobody seeing this picturesque island for the first time would believe that it was in fact the shell of a colossal sea creature.

As for the strike force, it was a sorry sight indeed. Three boats had been devoured by the baby krakens. Eight were floating upside-down in

the surf. Only one had been lucky enough to land in the water the right way up, and this was now a rescue vessel, puttering back and forth, picking up dozens of soggy survivors.

Erik Ahlberg sat cross-legged on the bow, wrapped in a yellow blanket and staring forlornly ahead of him. He had lost his feathered hat, his steel-capped boots and (for now at least) his insufferable arrogance.

Hilda, Frida, and the Wood Man did not attempt to board the Safety Patrol boat. They were lucky enough to be offered a ride by an alternative rescue vessel.

"Where will you make your home now?" Hilda asked the Lindworm as they climbed onto her back and shot off across the bay. "Will you go and live in the Great Forest?"

"No," said the Lindworm with a smile in her voice. "Living on the back of a Kraken will suit me perfectly. I'll have even fewer visitors than before."

14

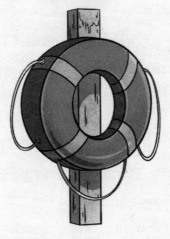

"Alfur, you're back from your conference!" cried Hilda, jumping off the Lindworm and onto the quay. "How are you?"

"I'm good," said Alfur. "I mean, I'm well. I mean, you need to come to the windmill. David thinks that Victoria van Gale is about to do something terrible!"

"Relax," said Frida with a knowing smile. "David always thinks van Gale is about to do something terrible."

"Does he?" said Alfur. "Well, this time he

thinks she's planning to use a ruby laser and a quantum accelerator to open a massive portal into Nowhere Space. Like you say, I'm sure it's nothing to worry about."

Before the elf had even finished talking, Hilda and Frida were off and running, sprinting side by side towards The Salty Maiden's bike rack.

When Victoria van Gale returned from town, she was surprised to find David tied to a post in the middle of the windmill.

"What's going on?" she gasped.

"Your creature went ballistic again," said David. "He's a menace, that one. If I were you, I would disassemble him and use the parts for something more useful, like the stuffing in a cuddly woff toy."

Unfortunately, Moss Head Fred was already telling his side of the story in a series of bizarre mimes.

"Bookshelf?" Van Gale frowned. "Hidden scroll? Oh dear, David found out about our little machine, did he?"

"Whatever you're planning to do, don't do it," said David, struggling against the knots that bound him to the post. "Surely you remember what happened up at the weather station. Interfering with nature always leads to disaster."

"Nonsense," snapped van Gale. "I'm not interfering with nature, I'm protecting it. Why do you think I want to open a portal into Nowhere Space?"

"Because you're as nutty as a fruitcake!" shouted David.

"I'll pretend I didn't hear that," said van Gale. "The reason I want to open a portal into Nowhere Space is so that people can live there. If we start building homes in Nowhere Space, we won't have to bulldoze any more trees and displace these poor animals, will we? Think about it, David. Why should nisse have that glorious empty space all to themselves? It's not right."

The scientist raised her arms in eager appeal and a sudden flash of lightning lit her from behind, making her look more than ever like an out-of-control comic-book villain.

"The storm is here," van Gale said. "Let us begin."

She took a remote control out of her inside pocket and pressed a single button. With a loud grating of gears, the ceiling of the living room began to move, opening up like the flaps on a cardboard box to reveal a mass of heavy machinery in the cavity above. It hung there like a huge car engine: a well-oiled engine block, a powerful battery, and an intricate jumble of wires and hoses.

What worried David most was the long, metal pipe that protruded from the middle of the engine block. "Is that a gun?" he stammered.

"Of course not." Van Gale frowned. "It's a ruby laser. It emits deep red light at a wavelength of six hundred and ninety-five nanometers."

"I see," David quavered. "That's all right, then."

Van Gale pressed another button with her long index finger. A leather harness dropped down from the ceiling space, connected to a jumble of colored wires. She carried it over to Moss Head Fred and slipped the harness over his head, connecting him to the machine above.

"House spirit, quantum accelerator, ruby laser..." Van Gale counted off the checklist on her fingers. "Ah yes, lightning conductor."

She stabbed a third button and David heard a quiet buzz high up on the windmill. It sounded like a metal antenna extending in segments to its full length.

Van Gale bent down and kissed her creature's mossy head. "Be brave, my dear. This is the moment for which you were created. Tonight, we make beautiful history!"

Lightning flashed, the windmill sails flew around, and a deep-red beam shone out from the muzzle of the laser gun.

The horizon blazed yellow, pink, and purple in the west, but the sky over Trolberg was an ominous black. Hilda and Frida set their faces against the wild wind and pedalled as if their lives depended on it, flying up the street like startled woffs. Twig streaked along behind with Alfur clinging to his stubby antlers.

"We should pick up Tontu!" yelled Hilda.
"Come on, this way!"

They crested the hump of the Bronstad Lane
footbridge so fast, their wheels left the ground.
Sheet lightning flashed ahead of them. Thunder
rolled across the rooftops. Furious weather spirits
piled up on top of each other, eager to release
their downpour.

"Girls, slow down, wait for us!" yelled Alfur.

Up and down the railway embankment

they raced, then past the Scout Hut and through a maze of terraced houses. Five minutes later they leaped off their bikes in front of Hilda's building and raced up the stairs to the second floor apartment.

"Mom!" called Hilda, bursting into the hallway.

"Hilda, where have you been?" cried Mom. "Oh my word, you're soaked to the skin! Frida, you too! Adventuring is all very well, girls, but if I'd have behaved like this when I was your age, my parents would have—"

"It's our neighbor, Mr Ostenfeld!" yelled Hilda, pointing down the stairs. "I think he's calling for help."

Mom leaped into action, as Hilda knew she would, dashing down the stairs and hammering on their neighbor's door. "Hello!" she shouted. "Are you okay in there?"

Frida was shocked. "I don't believe it," she said. "You just told your mom a bare-faced lie."

"I had to," said Hilda, rushing into the living room. "All right, maybe I didn't have to, but it's done now. Where's Tontu? TONTU!!!"

The house spirit's fuzzy head poked out from between the sofa cushions. "I disapprove," he said. "You just told your mom a huge great—"

"I'M SORRY, OKAY!" yelled Hilda. "We came to tell you that Victoria van Gale is about to use a ruby laser and a quantum accelerator to open a massive portal into Nowhere Space!"

Tontu gasped and all his fuzz stood up on end.

"Our bikes are downstairs," said Hilda. "Come with us!"

"No, you come with me." Tontu's right hand poked up between the sofa cushions. "Unlike your various other escapades, this one is an actual emergency!"

The four adventurers linked hands, arms, and paws, and Tontu yanked them into Nowhere Space. By the time Mom had finished apologizing to Mr Ostenfeld and returned to the apartment, all she found was a couple of puddles on the living-room floor.

15

Two girls, a deer fox, a house spirit, and an elf burst out of the drainpipe of a newly built house and sprinted through the wood. Horizontal, driving rain stung their faces and the howling wind made them gasp and shiver.

"What's the worst that could happen if we're late?" Hilda shouted.

"A massive rip in the fabric of time and space," panted Tontu.

"And what would that do?"

"It's hard to say for sure, but it would

probably suck the whole of Trolberg into a vast, endless nothingness."

Hilda saw the outline of the windmill up ahead, its sails a spinning blur and a mysterious antenna poking out of its roof. Behind the windmill, forked lightning shattered the graphite sky into a fiery mosaic. The antenna crackled and sparked, and the sails spun even faster.

Hilda sprinted to the windmill, wrenched open the door, and dashed inside. The scene that greeted her there was horrifying in so many ways: David was tied to a post, Moss Head Fred was wired up to some sinister-looking machine, terrified animals cowered in every corner, and a ruby-red laser beam streamed across the room into a crack in the far wall. She watched in horror as the crack opened like a startled eye, wide and pink and watery.

Victoria van Gale strode towards the portal with her head held high. She clenched her fists, gritted her teeth and stepped through into Nowhere Space.

"Come on, Tontu!" cried Hilda, rushing towards

the portal. "We've got to stop her!"

But Hilda had reckoned without the interference of Moss Head Fred, who stuck out his leg with perfect timing.

"Hey!" cried Hilda, sprawling on the floor. "That wasn't nice!"

Moss Head Fred picked up a pointy stick and hurled it like a javelin, missing Hilda by a whisker.

Hilda scowled. "That wasn't nice, either!"

Moss Head Fred sprang out of his chair and leaped on top of her, his hands reaching for her throat.

"Whoa!" yelled Hilda. "This definitely isn't nice!"

"Perhaps I can save you some time here," said David, struggling helplessly against his ropes. "MOSS HEAD FRED IS NOT NICE!"

Twig darted to Hilda's aid, growling and snarling. He sank his teeth into the creature's leg and shook it hard, scattering moss all over the floorboards. But Moss Head Fred was weirdly strong and completely ignored the plucky deer fox.

Frida was next to join the fray. She jumped

on top of Moss Head Fred, frantically tugging and ripping at its mossy head. Great clumps of moss and hair fell away in her hands, revealing something white beneath.

Hilda screamed, Frida screeched, David squealed, Tontu yelped, Alfur shrieked and Twig howled, all at the same time. For the head on Fred's shoulders no longer had a single scrap of moss on it. It was bare and gleaming—a grinning, chattering skull.

Frida was the first to recover her wits. She grabbed the skull in both hands and wrenched it upwards and sideways as hard as she could, allowing Hilda a few precious seconds to wriggle out from underneath.

"You go and get van Gale!" Frida panted. "I'll keep Bone Head Fred busy."

While Frida continued to grapple with the chattering skull, Hilda staggered to her feet and rushed to the crack in the wall, but there was now something different about the portal. It was contracting and dilating, and watery liquid seeped out around its edges.

It was Alfur who realized what was happening. "Fred's harness got damaged during the fight!" he shouted. "The machine is malfunctioning."

Alfur was right. The machine in the ceiling space above sparked and fizzled and the all-important laser flickered from ruby to puce to sickly green.

"We need to get that woman out of there," said Tontu, joining Hilda in front of the portal. "You should probably take my hand."

"Why?"

"Two reasons. First, in case the portal returns to a normal-sized crack when we're half-way through. Second, I'm a teeny bit frightened."

Hilda and Tontu linked hands and stepped forward in unison.

This was not like Hilda's previous experiences of entering Nowhere Space. Instead of the satisfying shoop of sudden relocation, the feeling was more of a bloob-bloob-bloob like swimming through jelly. And when they emerged into Nowhere Space, the wobble-walled tunnel looked even wobblier than usual.

Victoria van Gale stood a short distance away from them, marvelling at her surroundings.

"Victoria!" Hilda shouted.

Van Gale turned around. Her face was gray and sallow but her big eyes shone with childlike excitement. "Hilda, I'm so glad you're here," she said. "After all, without your insights, none of this would have been possible."

"Victoria, it's not safe here!" cried Hilda. "We need to get you back home!"

"What?" Van Gale frowned. "Hilda, I honestly thought you'd be impressed this time. You wanted to explore this place just as much as I did. You've been here hundreds of times. You said so."

"I exaggerated," said Hilda. "I've been here five times at the most. This space is not for humans, Victoria. It's not our world."

"And yet here we stand," van Gale snapped. "Hilda, I have a dream that one day we will all make our homes right here in Nowhere Space. There will be no more tree-felling. No more housing developments. Just peace and tranquility for every animal and bird on the face of the earth."

An eerie gurgling sound came from the windmill portal and a radio smashed at Hilda's feet. Then a coffee cup. Then a drinks cart, a record player and an armchair.

"I knew it!" cried Tontu. "The portal is unstable. It's going to suck the whole windmill into itself, and then the whole of Trolberg, and then, for all we know, the rest of the universe."

The gurgling sound turned to a rumble. The glowing holes on the walls and ceiling of Nowhere Space began to fade and flicker.

"Victoria!" begged Hilda. "Please, we've got to go!"

The scientist looked around with wide, frightened eyes. "I don't understand," she said. "My calculations were perfect. Where did I go wrong?"

Two startled-looking sparrows tumbled into the tunnel, followed by dozens of books and records. *Playing God for Experts* struck Hilda square in the chest.

Hilda held up the book for the scientist to see. "I'm guessing, you got quite a few things wrong. But we can talk about that later. Come on!"

Cogs and sprockets from the machine itself were now being sucked into Nowhere Space. Hilda, Tontu, and van Gale staggered towards the quivering portal, arms in front of their faces to protect themselves from flying debris. As Hilda ran, she bent down and scooped up the sparrows, one in each hand.

The windmill portal was already closing, as if being zipped up from bottom to top. Tontu leaped though the remaining crack, followed closely by Hilda and her rescued sparrows, followed closely by... no one.

Hilda staggered a few paces and collapsed on the floor of the windmill. The last thing she saw was Frida flinging the still-chattering skull into the disappearing portal, and then the crack was just a crack and the room dissolved to black.

16

When Hilda came to, she was lying on a
workbench in the middle of the living room with
a blanket over her. The first thing she noticed on
opening her eyes was that the ceiling above her
head had been closed, hiding van Gale's damaged
machine from view. The second thing she noticed
was that David was fanning her face with a book,
Frida was massaging her feet, and a mouse was
running up and down inside her pant leg.

"Eew," Hilda shrieked, shaking the mouse free.

David grinned. "Looks like we've succeeded in reanimating our patient."

"Don't even joke about that," said Frida. "Reanimation is extremely dark magic. I can't believe Victoria van Gale actually dug up a skeleton and—ugh, I don't want to think about it!"

"She was pretty over the top," said Hilda. "And David, we owe you an apology. We were too quick to assume that van Gale had changed."

"Don't worry about it," said David. "You two always see the best in people, and that's not something to apologize for. I think it's a good thing."

The storm was still raging outside so they all decided to stay in the windmill a while and wait for the rain to stop. They switched on van Gale's radio and sang along to a couple of songs to keep their spirits up.

"What do you think will happen to all these animals?" said Hilda.

"I'm sure they'll live here very happily indeed," Frida replied. "The windmill belongs to them now."

All of a sudden, the front door flew open

and two people in heavy raincoats dashed in.
The moment they pulled down their hoods, the
children groaned.

"What are YOU doing here?" cried Hilda.

"We could ask you all the same question,"
snapped Erik Ahlberg.

Deputy Gerda wiped her boots on the welcome
mat and stepped forward, glancing around in
obvious surprise. "The Safety Patrol's seismometers
detected unusual movements in the ground in this
area," she said. "We came to investigate."

"What's a seismometer?" asked David.

"Something that detects unusual movements in the ground," snapped Ahlberg, shooting him a scornful look. "So tell us, what's been going on here?"

Hilda's hand shot into the air. "Here's what happened," she said. "A scientist opened a portal into Nowhere Space, but her giant laser malfunctioned and the portal turned into a black hole, sucking everything into it. The scientist was harvesting lightning to power her machine, so I'm guessing that's what caused the trembling in the ground. We tried to get her out of Nowhere Space before the portal closed, but we failed. And then I fainted."

Ahlberg bent down so that his face was close to Hilda's. "If you're going to keep making excuses for marauding trolls," he said, "you should at least come up with more believable stories. Come on, Deputy Gerda, let's search the woods before that troll gets away. It must be a really big one if it's causing earthquakes!"

"Yes, sir," said Deputy Gerda, but as she turned to leave, her eye fell on the scroll lying face-up on the floor with a clearly labelled diagram of van Gale's machine.

"Deputy?" Ahlberg adjusted the toggle on his hood. "What are you waiting for?"

Gerda Gustav looked back at the three children and Hilda thought she saw the tiniest twitch of a smile at the corner of her mouth.

"Nothing, sir," she said, and they disappeared into the night, slamming the door behind them.

"Hey, David," said Frida. "Did you see what flew in when the door opened just now?" She pointed at a big bird perched on top of the step ladder: a glossy, black bird with a scarlet cap.

"Hooray!" David punched the air and reached for his camera.

"I'll do it, shall I?" said Frida, taking the camera gently out of his hands. "Might be easier that way."

While Frida set to work taking photos of the scarlet-capped warbler, David plonked himself down in an armchair and went to sleep.

Hilda felt a slight tickling sensation on her earlobe, which usually meant that Alfur was climbing into her ear.

"That was a great trick, Hilda," chuckled Alfur. "You guessed that if you told Ahlberg the whole traumatic adventure, he definitely wouldn't believe you!"

"I know," grinned Hilda. "Do you think it might work on my Mom?"

Enjoyed *Hilda and the Ghost Ship*?
Then don't miss the sixth book in the series . . .

HILDA
AND THE
WHITE WOFF

Catch up with your favorite blue-haired adventurer
as she meets new creatures and faces new perils in
the latest installment of Hilda tales.

Can't wait to get your hands on it?
Here's a sneak peek just for you . . .

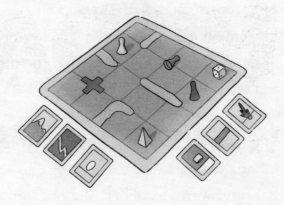

Rain poured. A deer fox snored. A house spirit gazed at a Dungeon Crops board. In the corner of the living room, a little girl with blue hair was babbling excitedly into a telephone.

"Frida, that sounds amazing... yes, of course I want to come with you... wouldn't miss it for the world!"

Hilda went into the kitchen, where Mom was busy spooning hot-chocolate powder into mugs.

"Sorry, Mom," said Hilda. "Slight change of plan. I need to go and meet Frida."

Mom frowned. "I thought we were going to play our new board game."

"Sorry," said Hilda again. "I do want to play Dungeon Crops soon, but Frida says she needs help with some homework she's got."

Mom poured hot milk into each of the three mugs and stirred it briskly. "Frida? Needs your help? With homework?"

"Don't sound so surprised!" laughed Hilda, pouring hot chocolate into a Thermos and slipping it into her adventuring satchel. She ran into the hall and grabbed her scarf and beret from a peg. "Frida says I can sleep over if I want to. Is that all right, Mom? Please say yes!" Hilda scooped up Twig and squashed him against the side of her face, big-eyed and pouting.

"All right," said Mom, "but I want you back here in time for lunch tomorrow, is that clear?"

"Hooray!" Hilda punched the air and twirled on her toes. "Thanks, Mom, you're the best! Come on, Twig! Bye, Tontu! Sorry about Dungeon Crops. We'll play tomorrow. Bye!"

With Twig at her heels, Hilda dashed out of the

apartment, down three flights of stairs, and out into the fresh air. She jumped on her bike and rode off, pedaling hard.

The rain eased off a little as Hilda coasted through the maze of apartment blocks and out onto Fredrik Street. As soon as she was on the main road, she leaned low over the handlebars and picked up speed. Twig galloped behind, ears flapping in the wind.

As she sped through the city gate and north towards the wilderness, Hilda did feel a pang of conscience for the half-truths she had told Mom. It was true that Frida had asked for help with homework, but it was witching homework, not schoolwork. And it was true that they were planning a sleepover—just not at Frida's house.

Frida and David were already waiting for her on the edge of the Great Forest. Their mission, Frida explained, was to collect dust from the ruins of Fort Ahlberg. Ancient castle dust was an essential ingredient for the invisibility spell that she was trying to learn.

The three friends hid their bikes inside giant

roffleworts and set off westwards into the trees. Frida and David carried huge camping backpacks and Hilda wore her smaller adventuring satchel. They agreed to swap when one of them got tired.

David had camped at Camp Sparrow several times, but this was his first time camping outside the city walls.

"What if we meet a troll after sundown?" he kept asking.

"Relax," said Hilda. "We'll have the castle dust by then so Frida can just make us all invisible."

"Exactly," said Frida, but she sounded more certain than she looked.

They came to a narrow river where canary grass waved in the breeze and weeping willows stooped to brush the babbling water. Hilda took a long run up, jumped through the air and landed in a giggling heap on the far side of the river. Frida followed and then Twig, soaring gracefully like a champion showjumper.

"Your turn, David!" they called.

David lowered his head and pawed the ground like a bull preparing to charge, but then he straightened up again. "Sorry," he said. "I don't dare risk it."

No amount of encouragement could persuade David to attempt the jump. In the end, they had to leap back across the river and search for another place to cross.

Half a mile further downstream, a pine tree had fallen across the river, creating a natural bridge.

"It's like a balance beam!" cried Frida, prancing across the tree trunk with her arms out to her sides.

"You may as well come back now," muttered David. "There's no way I'm walking across that thing."

Hilda took David's heavy backpack and gave him her light adventuring satchel, but still he refused to cross the pine tree bridge. "I'm slowing you down," he sighed. "I should just go home and let you two carry on without me."

"Don't be silly," said Hilda. "I'm sure we can

find an easier crossing point."

The walk continued like this all afternoon. David refused to use the stepping stones because they looked too slippery. He refused to take a short-cut through a glade of twisted yew trees because he imagined there might be a troll rock in the middle. Later, as the sun sank low in the west and shadows lengthened, his face turned pale and he jumped at every sound. Hilda tried to cheer him up by making up a river-crossing puzzle involving a troll, a goat, and a sack of grain, but this just scared him even more.

It was dark by the time they arrived at Fort Ahlberg. They shrugged off their backpacks and stood in silence, gazing in awe at the ancient, jagged ramparts and half-ruined walls.

While Frida collected dust, Hilda climbed the castle walls. The great, gray stones were pitted and scarred, offering plenty of natural hand and footholds. Hilda climbed quickly, except for one awkward overhang where she had to take her feet off the wall and haul herself up by her fingertips.

When she reached the summit of the ruined turret, she stood up and leaned into the wind, as high and free as a migrating woff. In front of her, the dense canopy of iron pine, birch, and bludbok trees stretched away towards the snow-capped mountains of the north, where a hundred troll fires crackled and popped.

"Be careful!" yelled David down below.

"I will!" Hilda called back.

As her eyes adjusted to the darkness, she noticed a pyramid of rectangular boulders poking up through the canopy about five miles away.

"Hey, guys!" she exclaimed. "You'll never guess what I've spotted. It's the Screaming Stones!"

How much can you remember from
Hilda and the Ghost Ship? Answer these
fiendish quiz questions to find out!

1. Which book did Frida press to
   get into the secret room's secret room?

2. What kind of animal is Matilda Pilqvist's
   familiar?

3. What is the terrifying plant in the Witches'
   Tower called?

4. What kind of conference does Alfur go to?

5. What TV show do Hilda and Mom watch?

6. What is draugen grog made from?

7. What is the Wood Man's ship called?

Answers: 1. Cauldron Care 2. A puff dog 3. A triffid 4. A grammar
conference 5. Trolberg Tonight 6. Sea water 7. The Nautilus

PRAISE FOR THE HILDA COMICS

"Pearson has found a lovely new way to dramatize childhood demons, while also making you long for your own cruise down the fjords."
The New Yorker

"Plain smart and moving. John Stanley's Little Lulu meets Miyazaki."
Oscar award-winning Director Guillermo Del Toro

"Hilda is a curious, intelligent, and adventure-seeking protagonist."
School Library Journal

"The art is as whimsical as the protagonist, and the bright colors enhance this comic book's magical realistic effect."
The Horn Book Review

"Luke Pearson's Hildafolk series mixes humor, mystery and fantasy into a superb piece of escapism for young and old alike."
Broken Frontier

PRAISE FOR THE HILDA FICTION

"A fun and pacey adventure combining a contemporary heroine with a gentle mythological element."
BookTrust

"Want to take the kids on a great adventure? Hilda is the one!"
The Great British Bookworm

"I have loved Hilda since the Hildafolk graphic novels, and now the full-length novels are just as good (maybe better)!"
Mango Bubbles

"Dynamic cartoon art brings the book to life, Hilda's bravery is an inspiration, and the world's details—the giant she chats with, the rabbit-riding elf army—will pull readers in."
Publishers Weekly

"The Hilda books are already beloved favorites of many kids; the Netflix series and these chapter books are likely to get her even more fans."
The Beat

COLLECT ALL THE BOOKS IN THE HILDA SERIES...

FICTION BOOKS

Written by Stephen Davies

Hilda and the Hidden People
Hilda and the Great Parade
Hilda and the Nowhere Space
Hilda and the Time Worm
Hilda and the Ghost Ship
Hilda and the White Woff

GRAPHIC NOVELS

Written and illustrated by Luke Pearson

Hilda and the Troll
Hilda and the Midnight Giant
Hilda and the Bird Parade
Hilda and the Black Hound
Hilda and the Stone Forest
Hilda and the Mountain King

Discover more of Hilda's world at
www.hildabooks.com